WALT DISNEY'S
Sleeping Beauty
AND THE GOOD FAIRIES

By Dorothy Strebe and Annie North Bedford
Pictures by the Walt Disney Studio
Adapted by Julius Svendsen and C. W. Satterfield

 A GOLDEN BOOK • NEW YORK

rhcbooks.com

ISBN 978-0-7364-3771-4 (trade) — ISBN 978-0-7364-3772-1 (ebook)

Printed in the United States of America

10 9 8 7 6 5 4 3 2 1

A happy bustle filled the cottage in the woods. The three good fairies, Flora, Fauna, and Merryweather, were flying about the place, as busy as merry, buzzing bees. For the first time since her marriage to Prince Phillip, Princess Aurora was coming to visit them!

So Flora waved her wand over the woodland flowers until each blossom glowed like a bit of rainbow.

Fauna worked her magic on the baby birds, teaching them to twitter a welcome song.

And Merryweather, with the help of the breezes, swept and dusted the little cottage until it shone with a magic glow.

It was in this very cottage that the three fairies
had raised the little Princess from her christening
day. And now she was coming to visit them here.
And they were to go on with her to the castle of
the King and Queen, to deck it out with magic
for the homecoming feast.

It was Merryweather who first heard the
clippety-clop of distant hooves and the rumble of
wheels on the royal coach, far down the forest road.

"Come, come, girls!" Merryweather cried. "She's
almost here. There's no time to lose!"

Quickly she bent over the well beside the
cottage for a glance at her reflection in the water
below. *Plink!* Into the well fell her magic wand.
But Merryweather was too excited to notice that.

Up bustled Fauna, puffing just a bit. "Oh me!"
she cried. "Do I look all right?"

Over the well she bent for a glimpse. But just then, the coachman's horn sounded loud and clear, off among the trees. So Fauna did not hear the *plink* as her magic wand dropped into the well.

Next came Flora, trying to be calm.

"The dear girl," she fluttered. "How sweet of her to want to see us and the cottage again. But remember, we must not keep her long. For the King and Queen will be waiting at the castle."

As she spoke, she caught sight of the royal
carriage approaching at last.

"Oh," she cried. "Is my cap on straight?"

She bent to look, then turned toward the road
as the coach came to a halt. And into the well,
all unseen, fell a third magic wand!

"Flora! Fauna! Merryweather!" cried a voice they loved. And down from the coach stepped Princess Aurora, into the good fairies' arms.

Together they went into the little cottage where they had lived for so many happy years.

"How lovely it is," said the happy Princess. "Just as I remembered it—and so are you sweet three!"

"Well, my dear," said Flora briskly. "Now we must all be on our way. For your father and mother have kindly invited us to come to the castle with you, and to decorate it for the homecoming feast."

"Lovely," said the Princess. "You'll decorate it with your magic wands. Where are they, by the way?"

"Right here," said Merryweather. "Why, we wouldn't be without them, you know."

"No indeed," said Fauna. "Always right at hand—"

"But they aren't!" said Flora. "Where are those wands?"

Well, they looked high and low, inside the cottage and out. But not a sign of them could they find.

"We cannot disappoint the King and Queen," cried Merryweather.

"And everyone in the countryside," added Fauna.

"We must find them!" said Flora firmly. "Now let's think. What were we doing last with them?"

"You were brightening up the woodland flowers," said Merryweather.

So they hunted through the woods. But Flora's wand was not there.

"You were teaching the baby birds a welcome song," they reminded Fauna.

So they hunted among the bushes and trees. They searched every bird's nest around. But Fauna's wand was not there.

"You, Merryweather, were sweeping out the cottage with the help of the little breezes."

So they hunted all through the cottage again. But the wand was nowhere to be seen.

Now the sun was sinking beyond the deep woods. At the castle, everyone would be waiting, they knew. What in the world could they do?

"I know," said Princess Aurora. "I'll ask the Wishing Well."

So over the Wishing Well's edge she bent.

"Why, it's all a-sparkle with sunbeams," she
cried. "And starlight and rainbows—deep inside
the well!"

"Our wands!" cried the fairies.

Tugging all together on the rope, they pulled
up the bucket in the well. Up it came, full to the
brim with magic wands and sunbeams and such.

Then into the carriage the four of them flew. And away went the horses, *clippety-clip*, off to the castle. It soon was aglow with sunbeams and starlight—and lovelight, too, for Princess Aurora's homecoming. And a lovely time was had by all.